Oddity

Written & Illustrated
by Kit Prosser

For my loved ones.

Florence Falconhurst
The Petal-Grace Princess

Woodland stands ready, to grow at her command.

A sweet scented kingdom with one wave of her hand.

Regent of acorns and ruler of flowers,

The flora and fauna all rise to her power.

Tor Kroll

The Mountain with Teeth

With scales as cold as bleakest night,

He crushes all within his sight.

With eyes ablaze with hellish fire,

'Devour them all!' is his desire.

Wing Commander Psyche
Of The Chrysalis-of-Courage Corps

For justice and valour in sapphire blue,

With the strength of many we rise anew.

With blades of grass we turn to fight,

Soaring to victory in bright crystal flight.

Grand General Scornhive
Of The Swarm Ogre Clan

Huge hulking brutes just spoiling for a fight.

Slobbering and slavering with evil appetites.

Born in their millions from a single egg spore.

Infesting our world, till our world is no more.

Oddity Moon
The Night Sky's Mother

'I'll cast the moon up to the sky with sacred, silver light.

To guide and rescue all lost souls who wither in the night.

My world is gone forever, my people's time is done

And I'll protect all things afraid from now till kingdom come.'

John Fright
The Quicksilver Trickster

When all falls silent in the dead of night.

When the moon shines cold and clear and bright.

Monsters flee and ghosts take flight.

Unlock the door and greet John Fright.

Augustus Falconhurst
The Monarch-in-Green

Bird of prey upon the wing, herald the coming of the king.

Benevolent ruler of this land, with the map of all creation in his hand.

From his mansion upon a cloud, he stands tall and he stands proud.

'O mighty sceptre of amber oak, I lift you aloft to serve my folk.'

Doctor Israkyr
The Designer of Despair

Wherever he treads, there's fear and dread

With no one left here to help you.

He's decided your fate, for you it's too late.

The shadow of Israkyr is upon you.

Gabriel Falconhurst
The Amethyst Emperor

'Gather beneath me, come do not fear me

For I shall make you all mine.

The Sun Crown shines bright, bow to its might

The might of my empire, divine.'

Merry-go-Rhonda
The Indigo Soloist

On the banks of the river, should you make her your friend,

Rhonda's sweet music comes from around the next bend.

A cheerful song of summer, soaring high on the breeze,

In clear crystal billabongs and lush indigo seas.

Look into the water and exchange for a smile,

A penny for your pocket, should you stay for a while.

Victoria Falconhurst
The Fate Weaver

Her star spiders twinkle, her kind fingers sprinkle

Their patterns and great constellations.

With fate up her sleeve, her many hands weave

The beautiful threads of creation.

The Hand of LAHI
& The Compendium Imagica

Hear me, O reader, mine.

The time has come for your star to shine.

Write your legend, it's yours to give.

Discover your dreams, they're yours to live.

You hold in your hand the power of creation,

A Limitless Abundance of Human Imagination.

Printed in Great Britain
by Amazon